W9-CAU-050

THE STORYBOOK BASED ON THE MOVIE

Based on the film
TEENAGE MUTANT NINJA TURTLES—THE MOVIE

Story by Bobby Herbeck
Screenplay by Bobby Herbeck and Todd W. Langen
Storybook adaptation by Katharine Ross
Illustrated by the GEE Studio

Based on the Teenage Mutant Ninja Turtles characters
and comic book created by Kevin Eastman and Peter Laird

Random House 🏠 New York

Copyright © 1990 Mirage Studios. All rights reserved under International and Pan-American Copyright Conventions. TEENAGE MUTANT NINJA TURTLES is a registered trademark of Mirage Studios USA. LEONARDO™, MICHAELANGELO™, RAPHAEL™, DONATELLO™, SPLINTER™, SHREDDER™, and APRIL O'NEIL™ are trademarks of Mirage Studios USA. Published in the United States of America by Random House, Inc., New York, and simultaneously in Canada by Random House of Canada Limited, Toronto. Motion picture copyright © 1990 by Northshore Investments Limited.

Library of Congress Cataloging-in-Publication Data
Ross, Katharine. Teenage Mutant Ninja Turtles. Summary: TV reporter April O'Neil discovers a group of crime-fighting, giant talking turtles living beneath the streets of New York City.
ISBN 0-679-80653-9 [1. Fantasy] I. The GEE Studio, ill. II. Title. PZ7.R719693Te 1990 [Fic] 89-43450
Manufactured in the United States of America   4 5 6 7 8 9 10

The parking lot looked deserted as April O'Neil, star reporter for Channel Six Action News, made her way toward her car. She had to admit she felt a little scared. After all, she had just filed her umpteenth report on the so-called "Silent Crime Wave" that was sweeping New York. All over the city pockets were being picked, apartments burgled, stores looted. Watches were being snatched right off people's wrists on midtown street corners in broad daylight! And here it was near midnight, on the downtown river front—not exactly a classy neighborhood. April was trying to figure out why the chief of police and the mayor had been powerless to crack down on these mysterious villains, when she ran right into a robbery in progress.

"Bad timing," muttered the thug stealing the TV monitor from one of the studio's broadcast vans.

"You're telling me," April said, gulping. Then she bolted, but the thieves quickly caught her, stifling her screams with gloved hands. April was so busy trying to squirm free that she didn't see the four huge shimmering reptilian shells rising up from the river like a line of medieval shields.

Whizzzzz! Suddenly a dagger came zinging through the air, smashing the streetlight overhead and plunging everything into pitch-blackness. Sounds of struggle exploded around April where she lay on the pavement. Who was getting beaten—her attackers or her rescuers? Then police sirens pierced the air as squad cars arrived on the scene. In the glare of the headlights, April saw the

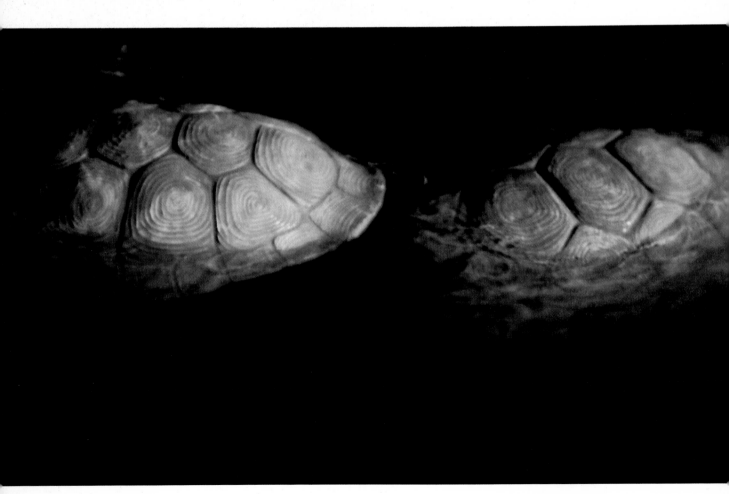

band of thugs lying on the ground, trussed up like Thanksgiving turkeys. Her rescuers had vanished into the night without a trace—except for an odd-looking dagger on the ground. As the cops arrested the thugs April hurriedly stuffed the dagger into her purse.

Beneath the streets, in the city's maze-like sewer tunnels, April's four phantom rescuers strutted along, congratulating themselves on a job well done.

"We were awesome, bros!" one said.

"Major league," agreed another.

They *sounded* like teenagers. And they were powerfully built . . . heavily armed . . . definitely green. They were the Teenage Mutant Ninja Turtles: Leonardo, Michaelangelo, Donatello, and Raphael—still cursing himself for having lost a dagger in the struggle. They burst through the door of their sewer home. For a sewer it wasn't bad. In fact it looked like the bedroom of any all-American teenage boy: posters on the walls, a telephone, even a TV. Except that this one just happened to be lived in by giant talking turtles. They stopped joking as they each knelt on one knee before another bizarre-looking creature.

"We have had our first battle, Master Splinter," said Leonardo. "They were many, but we kicked . . . we fought well."

Splinter was an oversize rat. Elderly and arthritic, and missing half of his right ear, he seemed wise and kind. "Were you seen?" he asked.

"No," said Leonardo.

"Good," replied Splinter. "For even those who would be our allies would not understand. You must hit hard and fade away without a trace."

Then Raphael rose and stepped forward. "I lost a sai, Master."

Splinter shrugged. "Then it is gone."

"But I can get it back. I saw—"

"Raphael," Splinter interrupted, "let it go."

But Raphael, the most intense of the four brothers, was not about to let it go. He had stayed behind just long enough to see that news reporter stuff it into her purse. When the time was right, he intended to get it back. But he said nothing. He merely seethed.

"I know it is hard for you here underground," Splinter went on gently. "Your teenage minds are eager. But you must never stop practicing the art of ninja—of invisibility."

Michaelangelo, like the others, had heard this speech before. And besides, he was starving. He went over to the phone and picked up the receiver, dialing the number by heart. "I wanna large, thick crust . . . with double cheese, ham, pepperoni, mushrooms, onion, sausage, green pepper, and *no* anchovies."

While they waited for the pizza man to deliver their order to the nearest manhole, they listened and danced to rock 'n' roll, feeling generally good about themselves. But Raphael didn't join in. He didn't feel like celebrating and he wasn't hungry. He put on the trench coat and

fedora hat they wore as a disguise above-ground and headed for the door. "I'm going out to a movie," he said.

Nobody paid much attention. Raphael was a bit of a loner, and besides, he was a big boy now.

Later that night in Central Park a couple of teenage toughs had just finished mugging a defenseless little old lady when somebody dropped down on them from a tree branch up above.

"Hey! What was that?" they asked, staggering backward.

That—was Casey Jones. In a muscle shirt and hockey mask, a golf bag slung over one shoulder, he was an eccentric, self-styled vigilante who was fighting a one-man battle against the crime wave.

"That was a crime," he answered. "And this," he said, pulling a hockey

stick out of his golf bag, "is the penalty." He lashed out and knocked one of them to the ground. "Two minutes for slashing." He tripped the second one. "Two minutes for hooking." And as he made ready to bring the stick down on their heads: "Two minutes for high-sticking."

Just as the stick came down Casey heard a voice behind him say, "How about a five-minute 'game misconduct' for roughing it?"

The voice belonged to Raphael, who was taking in some fresh air after the movie. Casey turned and checked out the trench coat and fedora. "Hey, Bogey, who died and made you referee? These lowlifes need a lesson."

"Not from you, they don't," Raphael said.

Raphael and the hockey player squared off. As they argued about which of them could better teach the muggers a lesson, the muggers themselves slunk away while they could still walk.

Early the next morning April O'Neil was getting ready for work when her boss, Charles Pennington, dropped by unexpectedly with his thirteen-year-old son, Danny, in tow.

"I wish you had called," Pennington was saying. "Maybe I'm odd, but I like to know when one of my best reporters gets mugged."

"I wasn't mugged, Charles," April said patiently as she combed her hair and put on her makeup in front of the bathroom mirror.

Danny sat on the couch reading a comic book, a pair of state-of-the-art headphones clamped over his ears.

"I tell you, it's getting so you can't even step outside in the daytime anymore," Pennington complained.

"Well, I'll tell you this," April said.

"Chief of Police Sterns is really gonna have some answering to do this afternoon."

The grownups were so caught up in their conversation that neither of them noticed Danny sliding across the couch. He reached into April's purse and removed a wad of cash from her wallet.

"How's school, Danny?" April came out of the bathroom just as Danny returned to his spot, innocently turning the pages of the comic book. Danny opened his mouth to answer but his father did it for him.

"Oh, *wonderful,*" Pennington said sarcastically. "So wonderful I have to drive him there every morning to make sure he *goes.* Speaking of which . . . we'd better get going."

Sullenly Danny slunk out the door after his father.

That's one troubled kid, April thought, staring after him.

That afternoon April O'Neil got her chance to put Chief Sterns on the spot while the Channel Six Action cameras rolled.

"No, I wouldn't say that at all," said Sterns, a portly man who sweated visibly under the lights. "We are presently executing a plan of redeployment that will minimize response time by maximizing coordination between patrol units in a decentralized networking scheme."

April looked baffled. "I'm not sure I understood all that, Chief Sterns. Would you mind repeating it—in *English,* perhaps?"

"It means we have everything well in hand, Ms. O'Neil," the chief said.

"Ah. Then you know who's behind these crimes," April said.

"Well, no, I didn't say that," stammered the chief.

PERSONALITY PROFILE

NAME: Leonardo
FAVORITE COLOR: blue
FACE MASK: blue
PERSONALITY TRAITS: unofficial leader of the group; disciplined; calculating; cool under fire
FAVORITE WEAPON: katana
FAVORITE EXPRESSION: "Slap me three!"
FAVORITE FOOD: pizza
PET PEEVES: anchovies, bullies, and pinheads

"What about an organization called the Foot Clan?" April pressed him.

"There's no evidence to link such a name to these recent incidents," Sterns insisted. "Now, if you'll excuse me, I have more important matters to deal with."

As the chief stormed off, April faced the camera and smirked. "We can only hope that *one* of them has to do with solving these crimes. Live from City Hall, this is April O'Neil."

Minutes later, April marched down the subway steps, fresh from an off-camera confrontation with Sterns. He knew as well as she did that the Foot was behind all these crimes. Why wasn't he taking any action?

"You expect me to waste precious manpower because a few Japanese immigrants in our city are reminded of something that supposedly happened years ago in Japan?" he had said. "Are you trying to tell me how to do my job?"

April was still angry as she pushed through a turnstile just as her train pulled away. Frustrated, she stood with her arms folded, little knowing that the Foot was creeping up on her.

"We've been looking for you, Miss O'Neil," a voice said.

She turned to see several men dressed in black ninja jumpsuits with hoods that hid their faces. Only their eyes could be seen. The one who had spoken had a definite accent . . . Japanese for sure.

"What, am I behind on my Sony payments again?" April quipped bravely.

"Your mouth may yet bring you much trouble, Miss O'Neil. I deliver a message," the man said.

He slapped her on either side of her mouth. "Shut it."

April reached into her purse for the dagger, but the men knocked it out of her hand instantly. Then they knocked her down, too, and she fell unconscious to the subway platform.

From out of nowhere Raphael appeared. Hoping to recover his lost sai, he had been following April. And it was a good thing, too. He was all over the Foot like a cyclone, clearing just enough space to bend down and pick up April. A train came thundering down the tracks. Seconds before its approach, Raphael jumped down off the subway platform with April in his arms and ran across the rails. He disappeared into the mouth of the tunnel as the train roared past.

"Are you *crazy*?" Leonardo asked Raphael when he arrived with the still-unconscious April. "Why are you bringing her here?"

"*Why?*" Raphael laid her down on the couch. "Oh, . . . 'cause I wanted to redecorate. You know, a couple of throw pillows and a TV news reporter."

Splinter came to see what the fuss was about.

"She got jumped in the subway," Raphael explained. "I had to bring her here."

"It's the newslady!" said Donatello.

"Can we keep her?" Michaelangelo asked.

But to Splinter this was no joking matter. "Herb jar," he said. "Cold washcloth. Pillow."

The Turtles went to do their master's bidding. Moments later, under Splinter's gentle hands, April revived. Seeing the rat, she shrank away.

"Acccch!" If there was one thing April hated, it was rats.

"Hi," Michaelangelo said.

Looking from rat to Turtles, April squinched up into a corner of the couch. "Omigod, I'm dead! No, I'm dreaming. I must be dreaming. Those guys in black pajamas hit me and I'm unconscious and dreaming. Where did you guys come from?"

"If you will please relax, I will tell you," Splinter said gently.

"Eeek!" April said. "It talks!"

Splinter began: "For fifteen years we have lived here. Before that time I was the pet of my master Yoshi, mimicking his movements from my cage, learning the secret art of ninja. When we were forced to come to New York, I found myself without a home, wandering the streets.

"And then one day I saw an old blind man crossing the street, unaware of a truck barreling down upon him. A young man dived and pushed him out of the way, but not before the truck swerved, tossing a metal canister out of its back. The strange canister bounced several times before striking a glass jar held by an onlooker's little boy—a jar containing four baby turtles!

"The little ones fell into a manhole, followed by the canister, which smashed open, covering them in a glowing ooze. I gathered them up in an old coffee can. The next morning, the can was tipped over—and they had doubled in size.

"Since I, too, had come in contact with the ooze, I was growing, in body as well as in mind. Soon the turtles were standing upright, copying my every movement. I was amazed at how intelligent they seemed. Then they spoke. More words followed and I began their training, teaching them all that I had learned from my master Yoshi. And with an old copy of a Renaissance art book, I gave them all names."

And so saying, Splinter introduced the Turtles to a stunned and speechless April. Each Turtle bowed in turn as Splinter said: "Leonardo, Michaelangelo, Donatello, and Raphael."

PERSONALITY PROFILE

NAME: Michaelangelo

FAVORITE COLOR: orange

FACE MASK: orange

PERSONALITY TRAITS: happy-go-lucky, wisecrackin' surf turtle

FAVORITE WEAPON: nunchaku

FAVORITE EXPRESSION: "Forgiveness is divine—but never pay full price for cold pizza."

FAVORITE FOOD: pizza

PET PEEVES: anchovies and people who don't like rock 'n' roll

Later that night the Turtles guided April through underground tunnels leading to the manhole directly in front of her apartment building.

"I'd invite you guys in," April said, "but the place is a mess."

"That's okay," said Michaelangelo. "We don't mind messes."

"But I don't have anything to offer you. Except frozen pizza," April added.

In a flash the four were out of the manhole and standing at the front door.

"You mean you guys eat pizza?" April said in amazement.

"Doesn't everybody?" Michaelangelo asked innocently.

While April heated the pizza, the Turtles entertained their hostess with tales of their life underground with the wise rat. Michaelangelo even did his impressions of Sylvester Stallone as Rocky, and a great Jimmy Cagney. After a while, April forgot she was in the company of reptilian mutants and actually began to enjoy herself.

"Will I ever see you guys again?" she asked, showing them to the door later that evening.

"That depends," said Michaelangelo, "on how fast you restock your pizza."

"Deal!" April agreed.

They parted feeling relaxed and happy. But on returning to their den, the Turtles found a nasty surprise. The place was sacked. Wrecked. And there was no sign of Splinter. When they saw the trail of blood, Raphael let out a cry of anguish.

Not knowing what else to do or where to turn, the four went back to April's apartment. She did her best to comfort them. The five friends stayed up for hours trying to convince one another that Splinter was all right. But who could have kidnapped him and why? Stretched out in April's living room, they fell asleep just before dawn.

A loud knock on the door woke them. The Turtles had just enough time to hide before a groggy April opened the door to find Charles Pennington and Danny. She didn't know which of them looked worse. What she also didn't know was that yesterday Danny had been arrested for shoplifting. Chief Sterns had struck a deal with Pennington. Sterns would go easy on the kid if Pennington would promise to keep his star reporter quiet regarding the Foot Clan business.

"April, listen," Pennington stammered as he came through the door, Danny shambling in behind him. "I've been thinking you should take it easy for a while."

"What are you talking about?" April's eyes darted about, hoping the Turtles had hidden themselves well enough. They hadn't had much time.

"I mean, look at you," Pennington said. "You're exhausted."

"I just had a rough night. That's all," April replied.

"Maybe you could use a little help . . . especially covering City Hall," Pennington suggested.

"Charles, don't be ridiculous," April scoffed. "That's my main beat."

At that moment Danny happened to look in a mirror. He caught sight of something green behind him. It *looked* like a giant turtle. He turned around. No giant turtle. That was strange. But there was no mistaking it. He had seen something bizarre . . . something extraordinary.

On the other side of town on an island in the river was a giant warehouse. From the outside it looked like any other storage facility. But on the inside it was something else entirely. What Pinocchio's Pleasure Island was to children this place was to rebellious teenagers. There were hundreds of them here, milling about, living it up, laughing, shouting to one another—in short, having a great time doing everything they weren't supposed to do. They were smoking, drinking, gambling, shooting pool, even playing knife games. Surrounding them, piled up high, were boxes and boxes of

stuff—stolen stuff. Anything that could be pocketed, carried off, or driven away was here: bikes, stereos, clothing, VCRs, watches, wallets. In one corner a group of teenagers in belts and headbands worked out on ropes, bars, ladders, and hoops to improve their speed and stealth on the street. In another they circled each other on mats, practicing the kicks and chop cuts of the martial arts. There were bunk beds, too, and lockers. It was a veritable den of thieves. Overseeing it all, with a body hard as cinder block and a face like a bulldog, his black dogi bearing a small dragon emblem, was Tatsu. He walked among the boys demonstrating pickpocketing techniques here, a flying roundhouse kick there, inspiring fear and respect wherever he went. Then a sudden dull buzz brought the entire warehouse to attention.

They stopped what they were doing and gathered around a high, well-lit platform where, hanging in manacles, looking beaten and exhausted, was the four-foot-high rat, Splinter.

A door swung open and a figure appeared. As he passed from shadow to light the helmet that hid his face glinted. A pair of dark, piercing eyes surveyed the crowd. A black cloak covered his body. The teenagers parted to let him through. He mounted the platform and seated himself.

Tatsu approached the figure. With great care he removed the black cloak. A full set of razor-sharp ninja armor encased the newcomer's body. "Master Shredder," said Tatsu, bowing reverently.

The Shredder addressed his rapt audience. "Our family grows. Soon we will break the confines of these walls. The city itself will be our playground to use as we please. There is a new enemy. Freaks of nature who interfere with our business. You are my eyes and ears. Find them. Together we will punish these . . . *turtles.*"

In the audience, little Danny Pennington meekly raised his hand. After coming here for weeks and being treated like a nobody, at last he had something to say, something that would make him invaluable to Shredder, something to prove that he really deserved to belong to this "family" of thieves.

Raphael sat on the roof of April's apartment building and stared moodily down at the lights of New York City. He had just stormed out of April's apartment after a bad fight with the others. Actually it had mostly been with Leonardo. They had been watching April O'Neil being interviewed on TV.

"I've spoken with a lot of Japanese-Americans in the past few days," she had told her interviewer, "who say that our recent crime wave is similar to the work of a secret band of ninja thieves who once operated in Japan."

Since the Foot most likely held Splinter captive, the Turtles' plan was for April to go on the air and lure them out into the open. The Foot would lead the Turtles directly to Splinter. But Raphael didn't like the plan. He didn't much care for using April as bait, even though Leonardo had insisted it was the best plan they had.

"So that's the plan of our great leader," Raphael had said, "just sit here on our butts."

"I never said I was your great leader," Leonardo had protested.

"Well, you sure act like it sometimes," Raphael had muttered.

"Yeah? Well, you act like a jerk sometimes," Leonardo had said. "And this attitude of yours isn't helping anything."

"Well, maybe I'll just take my attitude and leave." Raphael had picked up his sai and headed for the door.

Raphael was just beginning to cool off up there on the roof when the Foot appeared silently behind him. Suddenly one of them pounced and slammed him into a wall.

Raphael got up and dusted himself off.

In a matter of seconds they were all over him.

PERSONALITY PROFILE

NAME: Raphael
FAVORITE COLOR: red
FACE MASK: red
PERSONALITY TRAITS: Mr. Intensity; brooding and serious; has a tendency not to look before he leaps
FAVORITE WEAPON: sai
FAVORITE EXPRESSION: "I have an attitude?"
FAVORITE FOOD: pizza
PET PEEVES: anchovies, geeks, gacks, and people who look at him funny

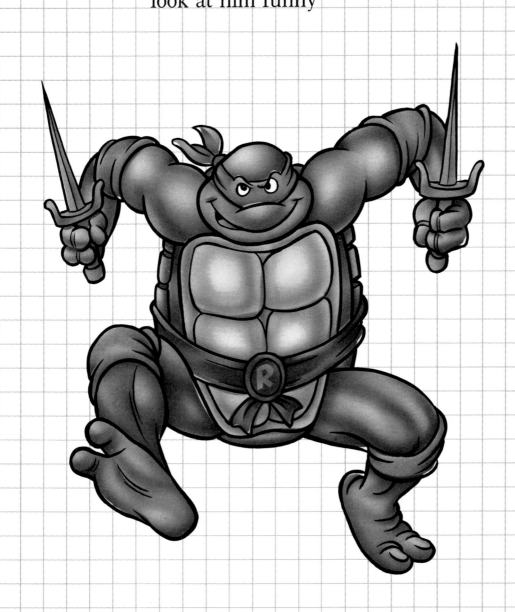

Down below, April had returned from the TV station and was getting ready to show the others her junk shop on the ground floor.

"It's not much, really," she said apologetically, leading them downstairs to the storefront. "I can only afford to have somebody run it part-time. I do it mostly for my dad. He loved junk." She laughed shortly. "I guess it's sort of silly to lose money on a business just because you miss your father."

Donatello touched her arm tenderly. "No, it isn't."

April switched on the shop lights.

"Wow!" exclaimed the Turtles. "Excellent."

"This place has everything!" said Donatello, digging in. It certainly did. Everything old and cast off—from used clothing, jewelry, and furniture to a stuffed polar bear.

As the three Turtles rummaged excitedly through the dust and cobwebs, a young couple came sauntering past on the sidewalk outside, window-shopping. The Turtles moved quickly to conceal themselves. Donatello dropped to all fours and pretended to be a table, which April promptly pretended to dust off. Leonardo grabbed some silk flowers and hid behind them. Michaelangelo stood up straight and stiff and threw a lampshade over his head.

The man outside pointed to Michaelangelo. "That's probably one of the ugliest floor lamps ever created by man."

As the couple moved on, Michaelangelo, from beneath the shade, pretended to be hurt. *"Ugly?"*

"Hasn't Raphael been gone a long time?" April said as she and the other Turtles returned to her apartment.

"Nah," said Donatello. "He does this all the time. He *likes* it."

Meanwhile, unbeknown to any of them, Raphael was being trounced, bounced, and beaten by the Foot up on the rooftop.

"Are you sure?" April asked uneasily.

"Don't worry," Donatello reassured her. "He'll probably be back any minute now, threatening to huff and puff and blow—"

Just then, right on cue, with a tremendous crash, Raphael's body came flying through the skylight and slid to a stop in the center of the floor.

"Raph!" cried Leonardo, dropping down next to his brother.

Badly beaten, Raphael lay very still.

"Is he . . . ?" April couldn't bear to finish.

"No," Leo said grimly. "He's alive. Barely."

Then there were more crashes as the Foot smashed their way through the windows. Slivers of glass flew everywhere.

"Whoa!" Michaelangelo said. "Talk about pushy!"

In rapid succession Leonardo whipped out his katana, Donatello his bo, and Michaelangelo his nunchaku as the battle began in earnest. April did her best to shield Raphael.

But just as the Turtles had their Foot attackers licked, even more descended upon them. The weakened floor gave way and everyone crashed down into the junk store below.

"Ooooooh!" the Turtles groaned wearily.

"We could use Raph right now," said Leonardo breathlessly.

As if in answer to their prayers, Casey Jones sprang into the fray with his golf bag on his shoulder. He had heard the ruckus from out on the street, and he was never one to pass up a good fight. Seeing Raphael, he hefted his goalie stick and said, "Nobody messes with my little green pal over there."

"Who the heck is that?" Michaelangelo wanted to know.

Donatello shrugged. "Wayne Gretzky . . . on steroids?"

"Attack!" ordered Tatsu.

"Eeeee-hah!" Casey cried, his stick held high. "It's Hockey Night in Canada." And he took out Foot left and right, loving every minute of it.

With renewed vigor, the Turtles helped by Casey continued to mow down

Foot. Then one of the Foot swung a bisento. It struck the wall, severing an electric cable and releasing a shower of sparks. The old junk shop began to go up in flames like a pile of dry tinder.

"We've got to get out of here!" Leonardo shouted over the fire's roar.

"Here!" shouted April, pointing to a half-door hidden behind a stack of junk.

"You coming?" Leonardo yelled to Casey, who was still slashing away at the Foot.

"You go ahead!" he shouted back. "I'll cover you."

While the others retreated, Casey held back the horde. Just as he got ready to duck out the little door himself, April's phone began to ring. Her answering machine clicked on.

"Hi, this is April. I'm not at home . . ."

After the beep, Charles Pennington's voice said, "April, look, I'm sorry, I don't know how else to put this. You're fired, April. . . ."

PERSONALITY PROFILE

NAME: Donatello
FAVORITE COLOR: purple
FACE MASK: purple
PERSONALITY TRAITS: intellectual; soft-spoken; full of childlike wonder; has a knack for fixing things
FAVORITE WEAPON: bo
FAVORITE EXPRESSION: "I'm not gonna pay more for this muffler!"
FAVORITE FOOD: pizza
PET PEEVES: people who think Shakespeare is a deadly weapon

Back at the warehouse the Shredder was plenty mad. His invasion force had returned in tatters, defeated. He stood over Splinter.

"What are those freaks? How do they know how to fight like this? You will answer!" He dealt a backhand blow to Splinter's cheek, but the brave old rat remained silent. After a while, Shredder gave up and strode off in fury.

Danny came slinking by. He had just returned from witnessing the fight: hundreds of Foot mowed down, that apartment building gone up in flames. And it was all his doing—he had told the Shredder about seeing the Turtles. It made him feel funny. Powerful . . . but a little scared. And maybe a little sorry, too.

"How can a face so young wear so many burdens?" Splinter ventured.

Danny turned and stared at the rat in surprise. "So you *can* talk."

"And I can also listen," Splinter replied. "My ear is open . . . if you'd care to talk."

Danny stared at him with a face twisted by doubt. "I don't think so," he said at last.

"Have you no one to turn to? No parent?"

"My dad couldn't care less about me."

"I doubt that is true."

"Why?"

"All fathers care about their sons," Splinter said, looking off and thinking of his own four "sons," the Turtles.

It was dawn the next day by the time the Turtles and April, riding in Casey's beat-up, wheezing old VW van, approached a run-down farm out in the country. Like the junk shop, April had inherited it, but she didn't get up here much.

"Well," said April, "this is it."

"Nice," said Casey sarcastically. "Didn't they use this place in *The Grapes of Wrath*?"

They carried the wounded Raphael inside the farmhouse to an upstairs bathroom and began to settle in. But first April had business to attend to.

"Can I borrow the van, Casey?" April asked him. "I'll drive to the nearest neighbor. There's no phone here and I need to check in with my boss and let him know where I am."

"The van's got a cracked block and isn't going anywhere—and neither are you," said Casey. "I forgot to tell you. Your boss left a message on your answering machine. I caught it on my way out. You're fired."

April sat down abruptly and stared at Casey. "I—what did you do, take classes in insensitivity?"

"Hey, I was just tryin' to break it to you easy," Casey said.

"Well, you failed miserably!" April snapped.

"You wouldn't be standing here if it wasn't for me!" Casey retorted.

"Oh, and what do you want, a thank you?" April said.

"Oh, no, it is I who should thank you for the privilege," Casey replied with a sneer.

"Fine. *Thank* you," April answered.

"Thank *you*."

"You're welcome."

"*You're* welcome."

As April and Casey stormed off in opposite directions Donatello looked after them fondly. "Gosh . . . kind of like *Moonlighting*, isn't it?"

The next few days were busy ones on the farm. Casey and Donatello tinkered in the barn with an old pickup truck while cheerfully swapping insults.

"Fungoid," Casey called out.

"Gackface," said Donatello as the truck's motor sputtered to life. He grinned. So did Casey. It looked as if this was the start of a beautiful relationship.

April sat around feeling a little lost without her job, drawing in her sketch pad and writing in her journal, recording her thoughts about her companions. Every day she grew fonder of the Turtles. And as for Casey Jones—maybe he was a little immature. But he was kind of cute. And awfully handy to have around.

Upstairs, Leonardo kept a constant watch over Raphael. More than any of the others, he felt terrible about his brother. After all, it had been their fight about Raphael's attitude that had sent Raphael up to the roof in the first place. What if Raphael never recovered? What if his shell remained dangerously soft?

Out in the barn Michaelangelo showed his worries in a different way. Brooding and withdrawn, he spent his hours in rigorous training, nerves on edge. He rained blows on the punching bag he had rigged out of an old duffel bag stuffed with straw.

Then one day things looked up. Raphael opened his eyes and said,

"Hey."

Leonardo scooted to his side. "You're awake!"

"What's a guy gotta do to get some food around here?" Raphael asked weakly.

"Hey! He's awake! Bring some food," Leonardo shouted to the others. "Listen, Raph, what I said to you before, about your attitude, I—"

"Leo, don't," Raphael cut him off.

They each put an arm around the other.

April and Donatello stood watching from the doorway. Donatello sniffled. "Guess I'm just a sentimental fool," he said.

Yet even with Raphael awake and on the mend, the Turtles remained at loose ends. They were still mystified as to the fate of Splinter and still up in the air as to how to rescue him. While the others puttered around, Leonardo went off by himself into the woods and began to meditate.

For hours on end he sat in his clearing in the woods, eyes closed, concentrating. Finally his efforts paid off. He heard a voice: Far off . . . a mere whisper . . . weak, but nevertheless as familiar to him as the voice of his three Turtle brothers. The voice spoke his name.

"Leonardo."

Splinter! There was no doubt about it. It was the voice of his master. Leonardo opened his eyes and sprang to his feet.

"He's alive!" he shouted, running back to the house. "Splinter's alive."

"We know, Leo," Donatello said to his brother patiently. "We all *think* he's alive."

"I don't think," Leonardo said dramatically. "I *know*."

PERSONALITY PROFILE

NAME: Splinter
FAVORITE COLOR: brown
PERSONALITY TRAITS: wise; kind and gentle
FAVORITE WEAPON: nunchaku
FAVORITE EXPRESSION: "Hit hard and fade away
without a trace."
FAVORITE FOOD: fish eggs
PET PEEVES: The Shredder

That night Leonardo and his three rather skeptical brothers sat around a campfire in the woods.

"If you dragged us out here for nothing . . ." Raphael said.

"Don't worry." Donatello whipped out a bag of marshmallows. "I'm prepared."

"Put those away," Leonardo said quietly. "Now, just do what I told you. Everybody close their eyes and concentrate. Hard."

His brothers reluctantly obeyed. There was silence, broken by the crackling of the fire and the shrill throb of the tree frogs. Just when the others were beginning to get a little itchy, an image of Splinter—transparent and ghostly—appeared wavering above the flames.

"I am proud of you, my sons."

The Turtles gasped.

"Tonight you have learned the final and greatest truth of the ninja—that ultimate mastery comes not of the body . . . but of the mind.

"Together there is nothing your four minds cannot accomplish. Help each other. And always remember the true force that binds you, the same as that

OK, NOW ATTACK ME! ALL THREE AT ONCE!

which brought me here tonight. The true force which I gladly return with my final words: I love you all, my sons."

The image vanished. As the Turtles stared at one another in silence their eyes filled with tears.

The next few days found the Teenage Mutant Ninja Turtles training with purposeful energy. From dawn until dusk they worked out. They trained with blindfolds on, learning to use senses they had not known they possessed. Yet they still managed to keep their usual sense of play. One game was called ninja hot potato. An apple was tossed about. Whoever got it had to fend off the other three while taking a bite and passing it on. When the last bite was taken, the game was over. After one such round of play, the Turtles gathered together, sweating heavily and breathing hard. They looked at one another wordlessly. They nodded. There was no doubt about it. They were ready. It was time to go back and take on the Foot—to kick butt as never before and rescue their captive master.

In the rattling old pickup truck the Turtles, April, and Casey returned to New York City, found a parking space, and made their way down the manhole to the Turtles' den.

"Great," said Casey, looking around. The place was still a mess from the Foot's invasion. "First it was the farm that time forgot, and now this. Why don't I ever fall in with people who own condos?"

"Sorry about the mess," Donatello said.

"I guess it's hard to get maid service when you live in a sewer," Casey said. "Why don't you try Roto-Rooter?"

"Quit complaining," said April. "It's just for one night."

"I don't see why we can't just get started right away," Raphael said.

"It's been a long drive," Leonardo said to his hotheaded brother. "And before we go out advertising to the Foot that we're back, we could all use a few hours of sleep."

"Yeah, I know," said Raphael. "But—"

A clanging sound coming from a cupboard brought everybody to attention. The Turtles drew their weapons and cautiously approached the cupboard. They flung open the doors.

"Danny!" April cried out at the sight of Danny Pennington cringing in the cupboard.

"Don't hurt me!" he whimpered.

The Turtles lowered their weapons.

"What are you doing here?" April asked.

"I ran away from home," Danny explained.

"Your dad must be having kittens." She made a beeline for the phone.

"Please don't call," Danny said. "Let me stay here tonight with you. You can call him in the morning. I promise."

Doubtfully April agreed, and they all settled down to get some shuteye. All except Casey, who wasn't exactly thrilled with the idea of sleeping in the sewer. He went back up to the street and tried to make himself comfortable in the truck.

With the Turtles snoring away, Danny got up stealthily. Tiptoeing to April's portfolio, he removed some sketches she'd made of the Turtles and crept out of the den. As he made his way across town to the warehouse, he did not know that he was being shadowed by Casey.

"I have not seen you for many days, Danny," said Splinter when he spied the boy wandering around aimlessly.

"I've been at my hideout," Danny muttered.

"And do you hide from your surrogate family as well as from your father?" Splinter asked.

Danny sighed. He was still so con-fused. He didn't know what to say.

"I, too, once had a family, Daniel," Splinter said weakly.

"Many years ago," he continued, "I lived in Japan, a pet of my master Yoshi, mimicking his movements from my cage and learning the mysterious art of ninjutsu—for Yoshi was one of the finest shadow warriors of his clan. His only rival was a man named Oroku Nagi, and they competed for the love of a woman— Tang Shen.

"One night, after Tang Shen con-fessed to Nagi her love for my master Yoshi, Nagi flew into a rage and began to beat her.

"My master arrived, and tried to stop Nagi. When the fight was over, Nagi lay dead.

"The clan's code of honor said that Yoshi must now take his own life. But my master felt he had done no wrong. With me and Tang Shen he fled to America.

"But Nagi left behind a younger brother, Oroku Saki. This brother swore he'd get even with my master. He fueled his training with hatred and became the most feared ninja warrior in all Japan, perfecting his skills with acts of thievery until he was ready to fulfill his vow.

"One night my master returned home to find his beloved Shen slain. And then he saw her killer. During the struggle, my cage was broken and I leaped to Saki's face, biting and clawing. He threw me to the floor and swiped at me with his katana, slicing my ear. But my attack came too late. My master Yoshi was dead. And I was alone."

"Whatever happened to this Oroku Saki?" Danny wanted to know.

"No one really knows," said the rat, "but you wear his symbol on your brow."

Oroku Saki and the Shredder were one and the same! Danny reached up to touch the headband he had put on as he entered the thieves' lair. Without saying anything, he unfastened the headband. At last he knew where his loyalties lay.

Then a harsh voice rang out.

"What are you doing here, boy?"

It was Shredder. Danny froze.

"Nothing," he said in a small voice.

"You're lying." Shredder's eyes, peering out from the sinister helmet, pierced him. With a single finger Shredder traced the outline of Danny's body until he detected the sketches hidden beneath Danny's clothing. Pulling them out, Shredder unfolded and studied them. Beneath the mask a cruel smile spread across his face.

"They're back," he whispered.

Immediately he sounded the alarm and began to gather his troops for an all-out attack on the Turtles' den.

"There will be no mistakes this time," Shredder told Tatsu. "I will go myself."

Tatsu lowered his head obediently.

"Tatsu," Shredder added, "the rat . . . kill it."

As wave upon wave of armed Foot poured out of the warehouse, Danny, lost in the crowd, hid behind some boxes. Then he headed in the opposite direction, back toward Splinter. He had to save the rat from Tatsu. But an arm reached out and hauled him in.

"Hey!" said Danny, struggling.

His attacker pulled off the black hood of the Foot. It was Casey, wearing a "borrowed" dogi.

"I've been looking for you," Casey said angrily. "You've got one heck of a lot of explaining to do, you little—"

"You've gotta come with me!" Danny said. "They're gonna kill Splinter."

Meanwhile, the troops of Foot advanced across town and began pouring down the manhole. As they kicked open the door to the Turtles' den they paused and looked around. The place was empty. Having awoken earlier to find Danny gone—along with some of her sketches—April had sensed something was wrong. She and the Turtles evacuated the place in time to avoid the invasion.

Just as the Foot troops were turning around, a gigantic blast of steam erupted, clouding the air and blinding them. In the steamy fog the battle broke out.

Moments later a large green hand reached over and turned off the steam valve. The steam cleared to reveal the grinning Turtles. And there lay a rather large pile of Foot. They never knew what hit them.

"Gosh," said Raphael. "I do hope there are more of them."

He wasn't to be disappointed.

A second wave of Foot broke in upon them.

"Oh, good," said Raphael as once more our hard-shell heroes got to show their stuff.

PERSONALITY PROFILE

NAME: Oroku Saki a.k.a. The Shredder
FAVORITE COLOR: black
PERSONALITY TRAITS: ruthless and vengeful; has a
brilliant criminal mind
FAVORITE WEAPON: bo
FAVORITE EXPRESSION: "Grrrrrrr"
FAVORITE FOOD: anything raw
PET PEEVES: Teenage Mutant Ninja Turtles

Back at the warehouse Casey and Danny had just succeeded in freeing Splinter from his manacles when Tatsu greeted them with an ugly sneer.

"Nghhhh." Tatsu stepped forward, assuming the battle stance.

"Nghhhh?" echoed Casey. "You know, a little Primatene might help clear that up."

Tatsu didn't laugh. Instead he delivered a punch that sent Casey staggering backward into a pile of boxes.

"That's gonna cost you, Tinker Bell." Casey rose and headed back to Tatsu.

Bang! Tatsu sent Casey flying into another pile.

"I don't think you're listening." Casey picked himself up somewhat groggily.

Boom! Again, into another pile of boxes. *Bang! Bam! Boom!* Danny and Splinter watched in helpless desperation as Tatsu knocked Casey around like a rag doll. Just when Casey was about to pass out, he looked up blearily. What luck! That last blow had landed him in a pile of stolen sports equipment. He picked up a twelve iron and rose.

"Fore!" he shouted as he swung, hitting Tatsu square on the chin and knocking him out cold.

Casey kissed the golf club. "I'll never call golf a dull game again," he said happily. Gently he lifted Splinter in his arms. With Danny at his side he walked toward the door. They were followed quietly by the teenage boys.

On the other side of town a manhole cover blasted into the air like a popped champagne cork. Foot spewed forth, followed by Turtles, followed by still more Foot, as the battle spilled out into the street.

Donatello and Michaelangelo were working as a team. In a flying leap they sandwiched one unfortunate Foot between their shells. Then, fighting back to back, they took on a dozen more. *Slash! Boom! Crash!*

"All right!" Michaelangelo cheered.

"Looks like this one's suffering from shell shock," he added as one Foot crumpled.

"Nah," said Donatello, "not very original."

"Boy, I guess we can really shell it out," Michaelangelo tried again.

"Too clichéd," said Donatello.

"Well, it was a shell of a good hit."

"I like it!"

The four Turtles backed up a fire escape as the last of the Foot invasion force drove them upward. Soon they were fighting on the rooftop. Suddenly a blur from an even higher rooftop landed in their midst. The remaining Foot pulled back. It was Shredder, come to take matters into his own vicious hands.

"What is that?" Leonardo asked, staring at the huge armored thing.

"I dunno," said Michaelangelo, "but I bet he never has to look for a can opener."

"You fight well," said the Shredder, ignoring their banter. "In the old style. But you've caused me enough trouble. Now you face the Shredder."

"Maybe all that hardware's for making coleslaw," Michaelangelo cracked, undaunted.

The Shredder twirled his six-foot, pencil-sharp bo and readied himself.

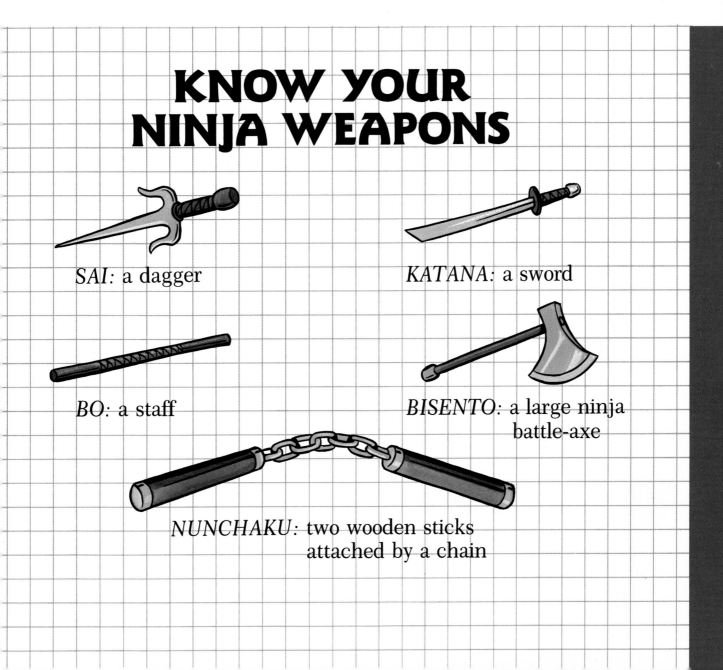

KNOW YOUR NINJA WEAPONS

SAI: a dagger

KATANA: a sword

BO: a staff

BISENTO: a large ninja battle-axe

NUNCHAKU: two wooden sticks attached by a chain

"I got him," said Raphael.

"Flip you for it?" said Michaelangelo.

But they opted for teamwork in the end as all four rushed him. With deadly accuracy the Shredder knocked them back one by one.

Casey had just arrived with Splinter and Danny. As he watched the Turtles get slaw-tered by Shredder, Casey said to Splinter, "Looks like your boys are—"

But Splinter had disappeared! Casey turned around. Where had the rat gone? There was no time to wonder as he watched the Turtles, breathing heavily, putting their heads together to reassess their situation. They hadn't even seen Casey and the others arrive.

"At exactly what point," Michaelangelo gasped, "did we lose control?"

"Maybe somebody oughta tell him *we're* the good guys," Donatello added.

"Any thoughts?" Raphael asked.

"Yeah," said Leonardo. "This guy *knows* where Splinter is."

"Ah, the rat," said Shredder coldly. "I know exactly where it is. We just killed it."

"You *lie!*" Losing his temper, Leonardo threw himself at Shredder in a rage. Not a good idea. Shredder was ready for him. With a few deft thrusts of his bo, he disarmed Leonardo. With the bo at Leonardo's chest, Shredder made ready to run the Turtle through.

"Saki!" a voice called out.

The Shredder pulled up. Splinter stood on the edge of the roof, miraculously recovered from the ordeal of his captivity.

"Splinter!" Michaelangelo called out. He couldn't help himself. He was overjoyed at the sight of his master. But Raphael put out a hand and held him back. It was obvious that their master had his entire attention focused upon Shredder.

"Yes, Oroku Saki," said Splinter, "I know who you are. We met many years ago in the home of my master—Hamato Yoshi."

"You . . . !" said Shredder, realization dawning upon him. Slowly he removed his helmet. His face was hideously scarred. Scars that Splinter had been responsible for so many years ago.

"And now," said Shredder, raising his bo, "I will finish what I began with your ear." An inhuman growl built in his

throat, distorting his face. It exploded in a howl as he ran straight at Splinter with his bo.

Rather than tensing for battle, Splinter appeared to relax. But at the very last moment, with lightning speed, he whipped his nunchaku out of his belt.

"Hai!" he cried, wrapping the chain around Shredder's bo.

"Chee!" The bo remained wrapped in the chain, but Shredder went off the edge of the roof. Only the bo, which Splinter still held wrapped in his nunchaku, kept Shredder from plummeting

the bo and reached behind his neck for something—what?

"For when *you* die," Splinter continued, "it will be—"

With the last of his strength Shredder pulled a dagger out of a neck sheath and hurled it at Splinter. Almost casually Splinter reached up to catch the dagger and in doing so let the bo drop.

Shredder screamed as he fell to his death, landing in a passing garbage truck. The huge metallic jaws closed over his still form.

"Without honor," Splinter finished, looking down.

After that, things remained pretty chaotic—but in a good way. The police arrived, along with Pennington and the Channel Six Action News team. When Danny caught sight of his father, he ran toward him. But when he saw April, he stopped and quickly counted some money from his pocket, then handed it to her.

"What's this for?" April wanted to know.

"Trust me," Danny said happily. "I owe you." Then he ran and hugged his father, who had been worried sick about him.

The police were asking some of the teenagers what was going on. "Go check out the east warehouse on Lairdman Island. You'll get your answers" was all the kids said.

"But April," Pennington was saying to his ex-star reporter, "I need you to cover this story."

"Well, I don't know, Charles," April said. "You know May Williams over at Channel Five has her own office . . ."

"You can have an office," Pennington said.

"She has a corner office."

to his death.

Shredder struggled to hang on to the staff.

"Death comes for us all, Oroku Saki. But something much worse comes for you," Splinter said.

The Shredder dropped one hand from

"A corner office," Pennington agreed.

"She's also the highest-paid field reporter in New York," April reminded him.

"And now *you* are?" Pennington asked. Having to pay April more money really hurt—but it was worth it to have her back.

"Well, you're a tough negotiator, Charles, but . . . okay—I'll come back," April said with a smile.

"Okay," Pennington said to his crew, "let's get her cleaned up! Let's go!"

A few minutes later, as April prepared to go on the air, Casey approached her.

"I've been lookin' all over for you," he said.

"Oh, hi, Casey," April said hurriedly.

"Hi? That's *it*? I stand here lookin' like I've just called Mike Tyson a sissy and you say hi?" Casey asked.

"Well, you don't need an ambulance, do you?" April replied.

"Well, no, but—" Casey began.

"Then just shut up and kiss me," April said. "I've got a report to do."

"I love it when you're pushy," Casey said with a grin.

PERSONALITY PROFILE

NAME: April O'Neil
FAVORITE COLOR: hot pink
PERSONALITY TRAITS: ambitious; has a soft spot
for hard news
FAVORITE WEAPON: microphone
FAVORITE EXPRESSION: "Give me a (news) break!"
FAVORITE FOOD: take-out Chinese
PET PEEVES: people who refuse to comment to the press

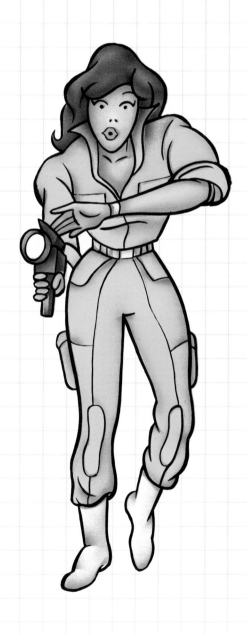

From high on a rooftop Splinter and the Turtles looked down on Casey and April. There was nothing like a happy ending, was there?

"All right, April!" said Raphael.

"All right, Casey!" added Michaelangelo.

Leonardo pumped his fist. "We were *awe*some."

"Out-rageous!" Michaelangelo topped him.

"Far out!" Raphael threw in.

They turned to Donatello, who struggled to come up with the perfect word to describe their exploits. But Donatello was at a loss. His brothers continued to top each other:

"Tubular!"

"Radical!"

"Dynamite!"

At last Splinter raised a finger and brought an end to the debate. "I have always liked," he said quietly, "cowabunga."

The Turtles stared at him, grinning, then laid down high-threes all around. "Cow-a-*bung*-a!" they cried in unison.

And the battle cry was born!

TEST YOUR

IQ

The Foot Clan is:
a. podiatrists who have a group practice
b. a secret band of ninja thieves
c. a toe fungus
d. a punk rock group

Baby Michaelangelo's first word was:
a. "Splinter!"
b. "Dada!"
c. "Ninja!"
d. "Pizza!"

The Turtles make their home in:
a. a big bowl with rocks and water and a plastic palm tree
b. the sewers of New York City
c. the Bronx Zoo
d. Beverly Hills

Which of the following is not a favorite expression of the Turtles:
a. "Awesome!"
b. "Far out!"
c. "Righteous!"
d. "Your mother wears army boots!"

Which ingredient had better not be found on a pizza ordered by a Turtle:
a. mushrooms
b. anchovies
c. flies
d. stink bugs

6. *What disguise do the Turtles wear when they go aboveground:*
a. fedora hat and trench coat
b. Groucho glasses and mustache
c. miniskirt and spike heels
d. ninja jumpsuits and hoods

7. *A dogi is:*
a. a pooch
b. a prairie rodent
c. a smoked sausage
d. a black jumpsuit worn by people who practice ninjutsu

8. *The Turtles got to be big by:*
a. eating their Wheaties
b. being slimed by a glowing ooze
c. working out at a health club
d. swimming through the waste discharge of a nuclear reactor

9. *A nunchaku is:*
a. what you do when you've eaten too much pizza
b. like a woodchuck, only furrier
c. a choice cut of beef
d. a ninja weapon

10. *Oroku Saki is:*
a. also known as the Shredder
b. a Japanese liquor made of prunes
c. Splinter's master
d. a chain of Japanese restaurants

SCORE YOURSELF ON YOUR TMNT IQ TEST

CORRECT	RATING
10	Cowabunga!
9	Radical!
8	Almost awesome!
7	Getting shabby!
6	Get with it!
5 or less	Sorry, dude!